Room 17

Pen Name:

Raphaël L. Marly

Pitch

In a stifling city, a man returns from Boston to face the imminent loss of his mother. "Room 17" explores separation, memory, and filial love. The hospital room becomes the stage for a final communion between mother and son, where each shared moment becomes a precious relic against oblivion.

"In the midst of winter, I discovered within me an invincible summer."

Albert Camus

Dedication

To my dear son Rémi, whose love for his grandmother will always shine,

To my grandchildren, Marcel, whom my mother was fortunate enough to know, and my sweet Alba, who will grow under the watchful eye of her invisible star.

You are all bound by this eternal bond.

Acknowledgment

To the one who believed in my dreams,

Delphine, whose presence and inspiration made this book possible.

May these shared moments and this outstretched hand never be forgotten.

Contents

Chapter 1

The Dawn of Farewell

"Life is long if it is well-lived, and short
if it is poorly lived."

— Seneca

Barely twenty-four hours after my arrival from Boston, that Sunday was stifling, overwhelmed by an unfamiliar emotion and an oppressive heat, reaching 36 degrees in the shade.

The city stretched out before me, a restless giant stirring under the weight of its own history. The air clung to my skin, thick with memories—some mine, some belonging to the streets themselves—whispers of unspoken words pressing against my ears. What life sought to convey to me stirred no desire to listen and would have defied any attempt at understanding. Denial is the mirror of the faith I cultivate—a faith born of my mother's hopes. Her fierce love of life and the faint hope that we might keep her among us. This "we" she cherished dwelled near the surface of her heart, resonating with every beat like a silent plea against the relentless flow of time. Each memory of her carried a permanence I couldn't erase, infused with the quiet glow of her unfading smile. And in that smile, I glimpsed the promise of renewal—delicate as morning light, yet impossible to live without.

In a somber performance, life leaves us in the singularity of one final, profound exhalation, like a whisper erasing the canvas of the world that saw our birth. Those who remain—the living—feel a chill of dread in the face of an irreversible absence. Our helplessness lingers in the silence, unspoken grief for what has already slipped away—proof of life's impermanence, felt more than seen.

In disarming tranquility, the soul gently sheds its earthly garment. It had been impervious to my naïve selfishness. My pleas could not disturb the serenity with which the soul ascended. This inevitable separation is like a silent river that, indifferent to the surrounding storms, continues its journey toward the ocean.

Chapter 2

The Echo of the Last Breath

"Life is not only what we have lived but also how we remember it."

— Gabriel García Márquez

The separation I experienced with such intensity represents the tragic counterpart of a universal reality: birth, that extraordinary moment accompanied by the natural and radiant joy of life.

The first breath of a newborn marks not just the beginning of life but the first act of separation—a sudden, inescapable rupture from the cocoon of the mother's womb, warmth giving way to the cool unknown. It is a passage, a piercing cry that shatters the reigning silence and, while celebrating the entry into this world, evokes a profound nostalgia for the lost refuge. Then, on the opposite side of life, there is death—that ultimate, harrowing, and painful abandonment that pulls us away from the endless dance of existence. It is the final separation, wrenching us from the embrace of our loved ones—a haunting silence that follows the tumult of laughter and tears. In this paradox between birth and death, between joy and suffering, the thread of our humanity is woven, where each separation becomes not only sorrow but also a testament to the love we have known.

My mother's vibrant spirit, woven with both melancholy and bursts of laughter, lifted her beyond the weight of her past—like a sunbeam breaking through storm-darkened clouds. Her smiles, radiant and contagious, lit up the darkest days while her laughter echoed like the wind through the avenues of my memory, infusing every moment with a touch of maternal sweetness. Yet, in the face of this inescapable fate—the feeble torch of our shared equality, a vibrant flame that would soon dim in the shadows—I became acutely aware of the absurdity of our human condition. In this striking contrast between the surges of life and the silence of death, only the memory of her love—an immutable treasure—and her boundless tenderness continued to flood my heart with its comforting light. Though fading, that light remained my beacon in the darkness, urging me to cherish each moment and honor the life she had given me. And within me, her presence endured—an unshaken star, shining in the endless night of my memory.

In its own way, the moment had been ceremonial and solemn. I intuitively knew that, for her, it had been so. This ceremonial essence was manifest in the simplicity of my being near her—a silent, sacred bond that lent a particular dignity to the moment. It was solemn, too, through the acute awareness that every passing second was precious, each heartbeat measured by the quiet litany of finite time. The subtle and intoxicating fragrance of the ephemeral surrounded us like a delicate mist, endlessly reminding us that life, akin to a sunbeam before twilight, cast a soft glow before setting. I knew that soon, death would arrive—not as a thief, but as a gentle hand, wrapping her soul in twilight's embrace and guiding it, with quiet grace, into eternity.

Raphaël L. Marly

The unbroken silence that settled around us became difficult to bear; it was so dense it seemed endless. I knew I would be the sole privileged witness to this final farewell—a moment imbued with gravity, entrusted to me by fate. The ancient phrase from old French suddenly took on a profound and moving meaning; in offering me her farewell, she entrusted herself to my memory and commended me to divine kindness. It was as though, in that instant, she sanctified our bond, entrusting me with the irreplaceable memory of her presence—one I would carry within me, always.

Chapter 3
The Suspended Moment

"You cannot find peace by avoiding
life."

— Virginia Woolf

Words draw the strength of their
meanings from experience; thus, the
feeling of their definitions is born. They
capture the subtle essences of our lives,
translating emotions into tangible
structures. Through their use, we sculpt
the contours of our realities, evoking with
every arrangement the mosaic of our
lives. Words, like wayfarers, travel
alongside us, shaping the paths where life

leads. Faithful guides, they illuminate the labyrinth of existence, shifting and deepening with every encounter, with every shared breath. They paint the blurred outlines of our memories and trace the sketches of dreams yet unexplored. In the unceasing mime-drama of letters and sounds, they become the guardians of our sensitivity, endlessly enriching the countless stories we carry within us. Thus, with every word spoken, with every phrase written, we redefine our inner world.

In this final breath, an expression once so natural seems to slip away, dissipating like a dream upon waking.

Room 17

Just moments earlier, words glided effortlessly across the sea of our thoughts, ready to be spoken without effort. Now, a strange pause—like a silent parenthesis, punctuated by three drifting ellipses, weightless as musical notes suspended in time. Yet even they cannot escape the unrelenting rhythm of seconds, ticking forward on a clock tuned with impossible precision. The ticking, like a lullaby, evokes the steady breath of a mother—a rhythm we would have wanted to eternalize, but that inevitably subsides, leaving behind a soundless void, an absolute silence.

Raphaël L. Marly

At that very moment, my mother's life slips away before my eyes; in a disconcerting immediacy, a wave of realizations engulfs me: the abyss left by the family generation that preceded me. The memories and stories, which had long remained dormant in the recesses of my mind, now surge forth, upending the certainties I thought firmly established. Every glance exchanged, every gesture now vanished, seeps into me. A delicate voice, barely a whisper, lingers like a fading echo, marking the moment as something fragile, now gone. And in its sudden absence, a crushing weight presses down on my shoulders, too heavy to bear. At this moment, cut off from everything, I suddenly felt a transformation taking place: I was more of a grandfather than a father and more of a father than a son. I carried within me the burden of ancestors—their unfulfilled dreams and regrets—like an invaluable load, both painful and vital. Time, in this turmoil, twists and stretches; an ancestral cycle emerges where roles intertwine and blur, tracing the threads of evoked spirits that merge with the current fabric of my existence. In this heavy moment, I realized how tangible the bond to those who had departed had become—like an invisible web, stretching from my roots in the past to the heart of my present, still unbroken, even amid the storm of farewells. Pain transforms into a bridge toward the unknown. There, I would learn to navigate between the shadows of the past and the promises of an uncertain future, seeking reconciliation with the legacy of those who came before me.

My childhood memories are intertwined with the heartbeats of my grandparents. I knew them once, back when I was still a child. To my youthful eyes, they seemed eternal, deceived by the slowness of time, as every moment felt like an eternity—much like staring intently at the second hand of a clock, mesmerized by the barely perceptible movements marking our sunny days and rainy afternoons. In that bubble of carefree innocence, where time seemed to pause, the world around us swelled with meaning. Every shared laugh, every story told, floated weightlessly in a space that felt both fleeting and eternal, as if sealed by the magic of the moment. From one era to another, seconds are twins; perceived through the prism of innocence, they seem longer. Each sigh of a grandparent, whose refuge was their wisdom and warmth, nurtured our imagination. That of the dream, with its light veils, made them more bearable, turning the trials of childhood into promises of adventure and wonder. Thus, my memories become silent witnesses of a time that is no more—milestones of an emotional journey I will never cease to explore.

Chapter 4

In the Shadow of Room 17

"And once the storm is over, you won't remember how you made it through, how you managed to survive. You won't even be sure, in fact, whether the storm is really over. But one thing is certain: when you come out of the storm, you won't be the same person who walked in."

— Haruki Murakami

My mother's final breath froze our shared past, sealing our family story with the mark of her exhalation. Our present ceased to exist; reality crumbled beneath me, leaving an abyss into which I did not know how to descend. My mother's sudden absence loomed like a menacing shadow, a cruel marker that violently tugged at the thread of our existence. Her last breath, a soft whisper of farewell, forced me to face a future without her—one that felt barren, hollowed out by absence, with only scattered memories to fill the void and a relentless nostalgia that clung to every moment. Without her, life had taken on a grave, oppressive weight, as though every ray of light was shrouded in a veil of sorrow. I did not know, even as I told myself, how to define this weight, for each reflection on her absence distanced me further from understanding my own pain. At that moment, I felt no desire to move forward, overwhelmed as I was by the vast emptiness and my sense of powerlessness. The unyielding void left by her absence was enough to measure the depth of my grief—a tide of tears I could not contain, surging to cleanse the inexpressible within me. Each tear fell as a silent cry, a tribute to the boundless love she had given us so effortlessly—gentle and unwavering. It was a testament to what once was, as my gaze turned toward a horizon shrouded in uncertainty, the future unknown and heavy with loss. In that sudden darkness, I found myself lost—a castaway in a turbulent ocean, clinging to the memory of a smile sheltered deep within my soul.

The child I still was in her presence suddenly became an orphan, deprived of his familial anchor.

It felt as though time itself hesitated, reluctant to move forward. That day, a Sunday, held a quiet kind of reverence. The sky was bathed in a soft, warm light as though the world, too, was pausing to reflect. At 6:40 a.m., the golden hour when night transitions into day struck me with the force of lightning piercing the silence, shattering the illusion of eternity I had clung to. On this day, August 20, 2023, the sun continued its graceful morning journey for another twenty-four minutes as if aware of the absence of a soul to illuminate.

My mother would never have missed such an appointment. She knew that God, already settled in His silence long before the first prayer, would offer her the precious solace of Psalm 23, to which she had always been so attuned. In that sacred moment, she found a quiet reprieve—a chance to rest, wordlessly seeking the absolution that would grant her peace. It was a hope for release, for a lighter soul, at peace with herself and with a gracious God.

Raphaël L. Marly

My mother was too devout to disregard the open arms of the Creator and His Kingdom, where the Eternal One—if He had not already done so— would decide the elevation of her soul and the course of her spiritual journey.

My brother, with an intuition as rare as it was unsettling, had foreseen the event with startling clarity. "She will leave on the Lord's Day," he had announced the day before, with a tone so calm it was almost soothing. His gaze, torn between worry and quiet resignation, betrayed an odd certainty—as though he were reading the pages of a book that only he could see, one filled with truths unknown to the rest of us. I could not help but marvel at the fulfillment of his prophecy.

The morning before, my son had come to fetch me from Bordeaux airport, eager to take me to my mother, who was already plunged into a deep sleep under the effects of sedatives.

With my son, time unfolded in a disconcerting paradox. It was too brief to truly savor his presence, to fully immerse myself in the fragile moment we shared—a connection born of raw authenticity. Yet, it stretched on unbearably; each second weighed down by the silent countdown triggered by my mother's sedation, a necessary step to end her suffering. This inevitable stage marked the conclusion of a will to live, now overshadowed by the mystery of infinity.

Chapter 5
Whispers of the Past

"The true generosity toward the future consists in giving everything to the present." – Albert Camus

Barely parking the car in the underground parking lot near the hospital, I rushed towards the exit and started running, closely followed by my son, toward the main door of the old Francheville clinic. I stepped aside, allowing him to lead me to the room, though he chose not to see his grandmother on life support. With quiet wisdom, he chose to hold on to the unforgettable memory of their last meeting, believing it was better to preserve that image of her, untouched by the inevitability of loss. The smiles exchanged between his son and his grandmother, a moment stolen from time, would remain indelibly etched in his memory. An invaluable gift for Mom, which he had chosen to offer by interrupting the flow of his daily life. This daily life that too many of us dare not interrupt, thus depriving ourselves of those essential hours filled with love and humanity.

We let ourselves be carried down the cold, sterile hallway, where every step seemed laden with the weight of unspoken emotion. The presence of the medical staff hung heavy, their practiced detachment a stark contrast to the vulnerability we felt in that space. My hand, placed on the door handle, made a slow movement down and gently pushed the door that opened onto the hours of our regrets. Mom and I were about to face that moment, starting with the one where we hadn't been able to arrive in time. The time that escaped us, the time I would have wanted to spend by her side in this room, number 17, which painfully reminded me of the day of her sedation.

Upon entering the room, I was enveloped by a scent of nostalgia, a gentle echo of the past. This somewhat crazy yet strangely soothing idea of turning back time seized me like an ancient whisper. Seeing her face, feeling her closeness, exchanging those words that only urgency knows how to bring forth was a balm I hoped for desperately.

In the sacred silence of the room, I imagined her gaze, overflowing with infinite tenderness—like a calm sea, its depths inviting both surrender and discovery, where one could lose themselves and find peace all at once. That gaze, a reassuring cradle, had accompanied me, comforted me, and gently rocked me through the storms of existence. Like an invisible thread, it had guided me until the day when the doors of time separated us. Today, in this room, the feeling of her presence was a soft embrace, a living memory.

It was like a dreamlike reality, where, for a brief moment, the past and present seemed to merge—each word spoken carrying the weight of ancient times, as though we were able to reach across the years and speak as we once did. When my eyes rested on her, I was confident that my singular purpose would remain unachievable. There would only be the urgency of my words to express, those words she would welcome with the scrupulous attention of someone who understands their gravity.

Her face, imbued with serenity despite the urgency, seemed absorbed in a deep listening, a listening that transcended banal language to touch the soul. In this moment of quiet exchange, there lay all that was essential. Each syllable carried the profound weight of unspoken truths, of understanding that could only be communicated here and now.

There, in that space reduced to the present moment, it was not just a sharing of words but a meeting of hearts, where the inexpressible finally found its meaning.

The echo of her breath filled the space, colored with shades that transcended the mere act of breathing. Each breath offered a picture of her inner state, a melody tangential to the inarticulate words. She didn't just hear; she immersed herself in the abyss of my thoughts, scrutinizing them with almost instinctive attention.

Chapter 6
Eternal Confidences

"Life is a temporary phenomenon, and the way we live it is what makes it precious." – Leo Tolstoy

It was not just an attentive listening but a true conversation of the soul, where words gave way to a palpable intimacy. In her silences, rich with unspoken understanding, she captured the emotions I struggled to express like a soft, intimate opalescence—an inner light that mirrored what I carried deep within.

Her emotions emerged, born from the intertwining of our exchanges, connecting us beyond verbal conventions. The space of this blue room was filled with tacit complicity, where every gesture and every imaginary glance became whispered phrases, witnesses to a connection silently weaving between us.

"It's me, Raphaël. I'm here beside you, Mom."

When these words passed my lips, they rose in the air of the room like an incantation full of hope. The moment seemed to halt, a final parenthesis between us, suspended in a presence as delicate and tender as the fading echo of a sweet memory. With a tender gesture, I sought to reassure her, to transmit the immensity of my filial love, to prove that this distance, although real, could never erase the powerful bond that united us.

In this simple and bare declaration lay the full force of my feelings, a chimerical cry aimed at piercing the veil of worry. Each syllable carried the weight of days long resolved—of shared laughter and tears, both healing and timeless—rearranging the very fabric of time and space to bring us closer once more.

Her gaze, a sea where surprise and love mingled, seemed to resonate in unison with my words. In this fragile dialogue, I hoped she would perceive the full extent of my presence and that this "I am here, Mom" would become a bridge between our souls, a safe refuge in the face of the world's turmoil, her world, our world.

These words, as insignificant as they might have seemed in that moment, carried within them the vibrating echo of an absolute love shaped over the years. Each letter resonated like a sacred declaration, bearing the oppressive expression of memories, fleeting moments, and promises unkept. They were the culmination of a life spent seeking to understand us, to love through the quiet struggles and wounds we sometimes inflicted upon each other—

unspoken acts of healing woven through the years.

Despair, like a heavy cloud, pressed down on us, the helplessness of having allowed misunderstandings to erode our communion between mother and son. How many times had we exchanged judgments instead of heartfelt exchanges? How many silences had we allowed to settle, digging a gap where empathy should have bloomed?

As I spoke these words, I felt a bitter mix of regret and hope. The lucidity of our shared journey struck me even more sharply; poorly expressed desires and unfulfilled expectations, all of which had shaped our relationship, sometimes with tenderness, sometimes with pain. Yet, at the heart of this complexity, the spark of connection always shone, this unalterable love that nothing could truly erase.

"You don't know me." This statement, delivered with devastating force, was aimed solely at me. It was one of my mother's last pearls of wisdom, striking and reductive, an affirmation that hit like a tolling bell. It marked an abrupt rupture with the future we had once dreamed of sharing—an undeniable realization of the silent distance between us, where our truths remained invisible, hidden in the spaces we could no longer cross.

This phrase was her way of extricating herself from a narrative I thought I knew by heart, a narrative interwoven with trials and embellished with fleeting joys. I had gone through so many seasons of her life, a keen witness since my childhood, but this sentence plunged me into a chasm of solitude and misunderstanding.

Chapter 7
The Sieve of Memories

"Life and death are but one thing, like the river and the sea." Khalil Gibran

A veil was drawn before my eyes, making disappear the exchanged confidences, the moments of complicity, to reveal a facet of her existence that I had neither suspected nor understood. I found myself facing a strangeness, a depth of her being that eluded me, a portion of her story that I had resigned myself to ignore. The pain of being excluded from this narrative mirrored back to me my own vulnerability—a quiet fear, born of years of shared moments, that despite everything, I had become a distant observer in the unfolding of her reality.

Perhaps not; these words did not carry the exclusion I feared. Through this concentrated expression of pain, perhaps my mother had nurtured the hope that I would accompany her, that through the twists and turns of her thoughts, I might draw the very essence of her being, that depth she had so tried to reveal to us.

In this quest for authenticity, she wanted to share with me her inner world, that complex place where dark and light aspects coexist, difficult trials and resilient strengths. Each syllable, each intonation, carried the weight of a struggle to articulate what so often lay just beyond our reach—an unspoken truth that neither words nor silence could fully capture. After so many years, she threw down a challenge for me: to see beyond appearances, to decipher the layers of existence, to embrace that vulnerability that, paradoxically, had made her so strong.

This invitation, as delicate as it was demanding, offered me the opportunity to reconnect with her story, to decipher the silences that had sifted our relationship. Thus, behind the severe words, perhaps lay the immense need for a more authentic, purer bond, a desire to be understood in all her complexity.

Her apprehension of life and others was of exceptional delicacy, a subtlety often hidden behind the stereotypes she used to protect us. By using these ready-made expressions, she inadvertently closed herself off, also confining those she loved into simplistic narratives, perhaps out of fear of not being present enough, of slipping away from the reality of our lives as she would have wished.

She stood like a family totem, frozen in time—an embodiment of a story everyone knew by heart, yet one that had lost its capacity to evolve, lingering in the past without the room to grow. Her image, solid and reassuring, never turned toward the unknown of the future; she remained rooted in the past, in those comforting memories that preserved our unity while cementing an emotional distance.

This duality, between her desire for connection and her inability to let the moment evolve, created a pervasive tension. Through her expectations, she sought to root our story, but in doing so, she risked depriving us of the promise of the future, of everything we might have built together beyond the shadows of her emotional legacy.

The apprehension of the future and its ultimate phase settled gently, like a fleeting caress, on the eternity of what had faded. Every breath of life lost, every act of love, left behind an indelible mark—tracing the outline of a memory that, no matter how deeply etched, continued to fade into the distance, elusive and just beyond reach.

Chapter 8

The Dance of Shadows

"There are only two things we must do
in life: love and learn to die."

Elisabeth Kübler-Ross

This shiver before the inevitable
brushed against the beauty of memories,
revealing a poignant duplicity. The
anticipation of forgetting, the extinction
of our exchanges, brushed against the
hearts like a shadow as fine as amber,
reminding us that love, though fleeting,
had managed to illuminate the darkest
parts of our existence. In this twilight
pantomime, the fear of an inevitable end

intertwined with the gratitude of lived moments, preserving the fragile flame of connections that, though vanished, left a persistent light—a quiet glow that lingers long after it fades.

Through this apprehension, I perceived not only the fragility of life but also the necessity of honoring what it had been, of preserving the essence of loved ones within the folds of my memory. In the heavy silences, in the lost gazes, the echo of our shared moments could still resonate, crashing against the walls of time, seeking to transcend the iterations of the past to project itself toward a future we did not know.

Room 17

She conjugated the future with the past as if to contain a present that always seemed to escape her. The past was her haven, a quiet sanctuary filled with bittersweet melancholy, where she sought refuge, her thoughts gently colored by the warm, nostalgic hue of memories that never quite faded. She would lose herself in these fragments of yesterday, reliving them with an intensity that contrasted with a present she struggled to fully grasp.

The future, on the other hand, plunged her into a waking dream. It was a blank canvas onto which she projected her hopes and aspirations, an escape space where every new idea came to life in an imaginary dance. She saw the future not as a logical sequence but as a deliberately vague, flexible promise where everything remained possible.

Caught between the melancholy of the past and the uncertain dreams of the future, she was perhaps searching to fill the aching absence of the present—a void that lingered quietly, just out of reach. This back-and-forth between what had been and what could be revealed a need to find meaning with time, a desire to harmonize these dimensions to make the present finally tangible and full of substance.

Room 17

Her melancholy gave her emotional depth, an abyss from which she drew reflections to protect herself from the pitfalls of anxiety, the anxiety of a future that, by its nature, slipped through her fingers. In this introspection, she found a form of wisdom, a refuge in the carefully preserved memories, where time seemed frozen, allowing her to breathe beyond the uncertainties.

The present, however, revealed itself as an insidious adversary. Each moment slipping through her fingers only deepened her sense of aimless wandering, as if time itself were a current pulling her further from where she longed to be. She felt trapped in a heap of worries, prey to a silent panic, unable to find her anchor in our present reality. This despair left no room for the serenity of the moment, and in this inability to connect, she became a spectator of her own life.

Chapter 9

The Watchers of the Dawn

"Death is so certain that one might even say it should not stop us from living."

—Marcel Proust

The panic generated by this erosion of the bond pushed her to express hasty thoughts, to react impulsively. The words came like shards of glass, sometimes sharp, sometimes disorderly, the result of reasoning rooted in diffuse anxiety. This phenomenon turned our relationship into a delicate battleground, where every exchange felt like navigating a minefield—each interaction heavy with tension as if a single word could shatter our fragile equilibrium.

Thus, between the melancholy that protected her and a reality that eluded her, she navigated a turbulent sea of contradictory emotions, desperately seeking a harbor in which to anchor, a place where authenticity and understanding could finally push away the agitation of her heart.

Mom had a fascinating and intricate way of reading the world, made up of her most intimate thoughts and the history she had patiently built. Every element of this framework carried with it a fragment of memories, unfinished dreams, and past pains. Through this complex web, she filtered the world, discerning the truths hidden behind our own masks, our own facades.

She understood us more deeply than we understood ourselves. In her gaze lay an unsettling intuition, a knowing that unraveled our certainties. Every flicker of her smile, every shadow in her eyes, revealed her ability to see beyond words—to cut through façades and reach the very essence of our souls. She caught the nuances of our emotions, those small vibrations that we sometimes had difficulty expressing, transforming our silence into a flowing language of empathy.

Yet, in her knowledge of us, there was a paradox. Despite this depth of intuition, we often remained prisoners of our own interpretations. It was sometimes difficult to grasp the attention she gave to every gesture and every word, the love she manifested in this way. At times, her past attentions may have seemed insignificant to us, lost in our own preoccupations. Yet we remained unaware of the depth of what she perceived and understood.

Thus, this web of thoughts became an invisible link between her and us, a connection that united us while shaping us. And, through her filter, a call echoed: a constant reminder that, even in our wandering, she was there, patient and vigilant, ready to welcome us with the understanding of a mother who had seen so much, who had accompanied our steps on the wavering thread of existence.

The 17th. On that day, there was no thought of postponing things indefinitely—it was etched into our memories, permanent and unshakable. It marked a turning point, shining with a special light, not scattered in the labyrinths of time. The medical clock, relentless and deaf, could not hold its breath, aware of the importance of the moments that passed with an intensity almost tangible.

A closed confrontation with destiny, an inevitable face-to-face, silently settled in. In the depths of this encounter, I imagined that every second woven between us transformed into a thread of gold, uniting two souls lost in the storm of their emotions. Mom and I spoke through the glowing screen—a video call that, despite its virtual nature, bridged the distance in an intimate, unparalleled way. Her face, bathed in the soft, ethereal light, radiated a quiet wisdom, a reflection of her gentleness and resilience. Every word exchanged became a sacred offering, a sharing of thoughts that, though brief, carried the weight of the years gone by and unfinished confessions. My heart beat in unison with the rhythm of this conversation, striving to grasp, to cherish every syllable, every silence full of meaning.

In this dialogue, we navigated through waves of emotions oscillating between melancholy and hope. Each spoken sentence drew us closer, like an attempt to reconcile with the past—a quiet, urgent plea for mutual understanding. That day, the horizon of our relationship brightened, even in the twilight, announcing a path toward acceptance, where words, though sometimes awkward, became bridges toward renewed intimacy.

This call preceded what would place her into a phase of solitude, homothetic to an eternal chrysalis. In this suspended state, time seemed to unravel, to vanish into the immaterial, like a held breath. In that fragile moment, as the distance between us grew, I stood before her, my heart quietly unfolding in an unspoken farewell.

The words remained firmly anchored in my throat, birthed from a silent sorrow that infiltrated every thought. Purple tears, shining like rubies, escaped, revealing the sacredness of a moment where everything shrank to the essentials. This secret, this last breath of love, asserted itself as a necessity. "I love you, Mom," I whispered, the sound of my voice trembling like a fragile autumn leaf in the wind.

She looked at me intensely, surrounded by my brothers, beyond anything that could be expressed in words. The words, for her, blossomed softly: "I love you too, my boy, I love you all." In this shared promise, there, in the midst of sorrow, resided a persistent light.

The words created a cocoon of warmth around us, enveloping us in infinite tenderness, like an invisible embrace.

This moment, though heavy with sorrowful tears, was also a quiet celebration of our love—of all we had been and all we would forever remain to her. In this ever-shifting connection, we created a sanctuary, a space where tears and smiles intertwined, where every "I love you" carried a promise of permanence beyond words.

Her gaze and her smile evoked those of the past when, as a child, I needed comfort. At that moment, I finally found her again, her enchanting presence rekindling in my memories as warm as the rays of the sun at dawn. Yet, within this sweetness, a paradox settled, for I knew I was losing her inexorably.

Her image, at that instant, took on an unusual serenity, marked by new wisdom, as if the trials she had faced had led her to a state of grace at the threshold of the inevitable. Every expression on her face told a story—whispers of past struggles and quiet victories, a mosaic of life intricately woven with love and courage.

I felt that, in this final encounter, she was offering me an unprecedented gift: the chance to grasp the essence of her being, to recognize the quiet strength that animated her. Far from the anguish one might imagine when approaching the end, there was in her gaze a comforting clarity, an invitation to embrace the journey we had shared, to celebrate the beauty of our shared memories.

As I watched her, I realized that this separation, though painful, was also a continuation. Beyond the body, our bond would remain vibrant and luminous, like a golden thread weaving through time. And in that thought, I found a semblance of peace—a quiet promise that, even in her absence, her presence would remain woven into the fabric of my being.

The real becomes unreal and becomes indescribable. In the wake of this transformation, the contours of existence blur, and memories and perceptions merge into a perceptible mist. Familiarity fades, giving way to a sense of strangeness, as if the world is slipping away beneath my feet, reinventing itself at every moment in the invisible.

It is a troubling experience where every once tangible detail dissipates, revealing the absurd beauty of what surrounds us. Fragments of life, a fleeting brilliance, become fleeing shadows, mere impressions, left as trompe-l'œil by a time that eludes us. Voices, once bright and full of laughter, fade into murmurs—brushing the ear like a whispering breeze, carried away by the echoes of a forgotten melody.

In this parallel, I find myself caught between regret and wonder, scanning these vanished moments that seem to slip like grains of sand through my fingers. This vertigo invites me to explore the winding paths of my being, pushing open the doors of the invisible, where the inexplicable blossoms and finds its meaning. This fragment of the tangible becomes a stage for my thoughts—a sacred space where I learn to navigate the unreal, to seek out a star even in the deepest darkness.

Thus, when the real becomes unreal, I discover with awe the intensity of each moment, aware that what cannot be defined paradoxically becomes richer and truer. Emotions, shadows, and light create the canvas of a vibrant humanity, living fully despite its uncertainties.

It is impossible to make a final realization: a last glance, a last smile, a last expression on the face. Every moment was filled with the terrible awareness that her silhouette loomed at the edge of her mind, like a faltering shadow, oscillating between the tangible and the intangible. Her being, so close, seemed to gently incline toward the shadow of her soul, a silent goodbye rippling in the air, heavy with unspoken emotions.

In this suspended moment, an exchange of invisible bonds united our souls to one another, recalling promises whispered in the corners of memories. The heartbreaking intensity of this separation only amplified the beauty of the moment between absence and presence, between what was and what could be. This final moment, captured with piercing clarity, intertwined with a first—the first moment without her—forming a space where pain and gratitude wavered in fragile balance.

The twilight, that moment when day gives way to night, symbolizes life. The lightness of memories intertwined with the sadness of the inevitable. Each filament, each nuance of light, told the story of a passage, of a love that will endure even in absence.

This twilight of the evening of a life was not merely a conclusion but blossomed into a promise, a promise that the essence of what had been would forever reside in the interstices of my heart. In this spiritual embrace, time dilated, and I knew, deep within myself, that beyond this final exchange, love, in its purest form, would transcend separation, nourished by memories, illuminating shadows with its unwavering warmth.

I find myself endlessly and silently reliving that moment—watching as Mom's chest emptied of its final breath, like a dizzying fall from which she could never rise. It was a scene both haunting and immense, a seismic rupture in my soul—a tragic masterpiece shaped by life's own fading breath. The steady beats of her heart echoed again and again in my mind while emotion overwhelmed me, shaking my entire being in the face of this harsh reality.

How can God breathe life into us only to withdraw it with such extremism? This troubling question still resounds within me, like a mournful melody repeated in a loop. I search the sky, seeking answers to this act—both divine and cruel—to this long-dreaded passage into the unknown. What does it truly mean, and why are we so profoundly unprepared for it?

Losing the one who carried, accompanied, and loved me places me in a painful void, an abyss of uncertainty where meaning crumbles. There is a duality in this trial, a destabilizing contrast between the love that blossoms in memory and the loss, which draws me into its darkness. What should we fear in this definitive separation? Is it the pain of emptiness, the broken bonds, or the loneliness that creeps into the corners of my heart?

And what should I expect from it? Perhaps it is a kind of comfort, a soothing, a reconciliation with what was and is no more. Accepting that life, in all its fleeting beauty, also seeks to teach me resilience—a quiet, unshakable strength. In this moment of heartbreak, between the breath that fades and the memories that endure, I begin to see that the bonds forged by love never truly disappear. They transform, adapt, and find new ways to exist, even in their absence.

This journey, though tumultuous inwardly, becomes a path toward the light, where each pain carries within it the seed of eternal memory, a tribute to the one who gave me life, even and especially when her breath left her.

Would an explanation remove the anxiety of the unknown and ignorance? Like a child afraid of the dark, the depth of an unpredictable sleep into which he will fall anyway. In this struggle against anxiety, I search for answers and clarifications that might soothe my fears and dispel the shadows of the unknown that weigh on my heart.

Yet, like that child facing the night, there is a troubling beauty in this apprehension. The unknown, the mystery, also holds unsuspected promises. Dreams themselves seem to hold quiet magic—flashes of light piercing the darkness, weaving enchanting tales that stir the imagination and gently mend unseen wounds. Judging by the serene expression of her angelic face, dreams are windows opened to a world where anything becomes possible, where the pains of reality dissipate.

Room 17

We, the observers, dive into this scene with all the tenderness our gaze can offer. Every smile, every sigh of the sleeping child becomes a promise, a reminder that peace is sometimes found where the mind escapes. In this gentle surrender, the child seems to go to meet the angels.

Over the weeks and months, my tears have turned to blue ink—the color of the sky, an infinite hue in which she now eternally resides. Each drop shed, each sorrow endured, has become part of this celestial trace, a testament to the life that was hers and the love that remains. This blue ink floats in the azure, a symbol of peace that I hope for her, where her soul can blossom freely, far from the world's pains. In this vast sky, she has become a thread of light, weaving through the clouds, illuminating the dark days of this earth we continue to walk. I imagine her up there, at peace, vibrating with the serenity that only the suffering of separation can offer.

And in the space she now occupies, where horizons expand, I feel the sweetness of her memories caressing my heart. Every chuckle she shared, every glance exchanged, is etched like stars in this deep navy sky. They shine not only with nostalgia but with gratitude—

for the moments we lived, for the unbreakable bond that threads the past into the present.

In this celestial place, I affirm my promise: to keep her memory alive through the lives that surround her. To continue sharing her laughter, her love, in every daily gesture, so that the drops of this blue ink never fade for anything in the world. For where she rests, in this ocean of azure, is the certainty that her soul remains alive, that her spirit wanders through these vast skies, wrapped in the tranquility we wished for her.

Thus, I find comfort in the idea that, despite the loss, there exists a connection, an alchemy between the visible and the invisible, between her and me. A gentle promise: she still lives in me through every glimmer of light in this blue sky, every cloud whose wind, in its majestic creativity, draws shapes and signs from her.

A peace I could never grasp, an inner quest I pursued relentlessly yet failed to reach. The emptiness echoed within me—a hollow reverberation of uncertainty in the face of life's greatest mystery: death. It stood before me, fascinating, wrapped in the eternal wisdom that eluded me.

Room 17

Each step toward acceptance was a step into the unknown. Death, though inevitable, had a way of highlighting the fragility of my existence, like a distorting mirror that betrayed my fears, my unfulfilled desires, and my fleeting memories. In my solitary reflections, I confronted a relentless reality: how does one find serenity in the departure of those we love most?

This question followed me like an unchanging shadow. Accepting it, the end of a cycle, gave me the impression of building a wall between happiness and me. The rituals of life, all that once warmed my heart, became painful reminders of what had been and what would no longer be. I desperately sought a key to unlock peace—a thread of meaning that could weave my sorrow into a living gratitude.

Thus, I realized that this quest was intrinsically tied to my relationship with life itself. Accepting death as an inherent component of existence is to recognize the fleeting beauty of the moments shared. Death should not be seen as a final point but rather as a kind of rebirth, an invitation to celebrate precious moments, to cherish every smile, and to embrace every embrace.

Room 17

Perhaps the peace I sought did not lie in a complete understanding of death but rather in the ability to welcome all that accompanies it: joy, pain, memories.

It was a dance between shadow and light—an acceptance of life's cycles, urging me to embrace each moment fully with those who remain.

So, by confronting this mystery, I began to see death not as an end but as a path to a new form of connection, a way to perpetuate love through every action and every thought. A promise of life beyond words, where peace is born from this complex mix of emotions at the heart of a vibrant and eternal humanity.

Raphaël L. Marly

I had entered the night of Room 17, carried by the serenity of an inexplicable faith and the idea of a probable miracle. In retrospect, this belief seemed absurd, almost naïve, but at the time, it heightened my presence with her. Every second became imbued with a new depth, justifying my being by her side through the night, through the end of her life.

We had time and silence to share as we awaited her unwelcome absence— a precious gift within an inescapable truth. These moments, though heavy with melancholy, became a sacred space, a cocoon where past and present intertwined, allowing us to reflect, cherish, and quietly celebrate all that we had been together. Each word, each glance toward her, became a star shining in the darkness, illuminating the path we walked side by side.

This shared space was meant to reassure her while confronting me with the challenge of time. Time, now a sandglass, manifested before my eyes: the amount of sand was invisible, but its flow was perceptible, a relentless current reminding me of the inevitability of our journey. Each grain of sand, each passing minute, signaled not just the closing of a chapter but the awakening of a deeper awareness—the enduring, unconditional love that bound us forever.

Between the present moment and memory, I found myself learning to embrace each emotion, to accept the bitterness of reality. While knowing that every moment spent together was a treasure, I let myself be lulled by the tranquility of our connection, hopeful for a miracle hidden in the intervals of the invisible, perhaps even a final reflection of light casting a backlit image of our intertwined lives.

Thus, in Room 17, enveloped by the night, we inscribed our story into the great book of existence—illuminating the final act of our shared journey with the quiet radiance of a faith that, despite everything, endures.

An olive wood cross, crafted in Bethlehem, the birthplace of the Son, found refuge in the palm of my left hand. This symbol, full of meaning and mystery, shared all my nights for months, embedding itself in the fabric of my thoughts, and during the day, it seldom left me. It had become a reassuring presence, a talisman against anxiety, pain, and oblivion.

I did not yet realize that she and I would walk together in the shadow of Mom—that our paths would intertwine so profoundly, forging an extraordinary and mystical bond, a connection beyond time. With every moment spent by her side, I felt a more intense bond, a precarious yet powerful balance shaped by love, memory, and that sense of transcendence the cross seemed to evoke.

In moments of doubt, when uncertainty pressed too heavily upon me, I reached for it—tracing my fingers over the warm wood as if to remind myself that faith can manifest in the most unexpected forms. This cross, representing a history rich with symbols, became a silent witness to our journey. It expressed the strength of our bonds, uniting our love with the one that transcends time and space.

When I was with Mom, the cross became the thread of Ariadne that ultimately united our existences, linking her story to mine and inviting us to explore the depths of our relationship. Every shared silence nourished itself with this symbolic power, giving exceptional meaning to our presence, transcended by the existence of this cross.

Through this sacred union, I came to understand that love, in its purest form, has the power to lift us beyond our trials—casting a gentle, unwavering light, even in the depths of our darkest moments. The cross, then, became the symbol of our shared resilience, a reminder that every suffering can transform into strength and that every obstacle on our path is an opportunity to grow together, hand in hand, heart to heart.

I had anticipated the dawn from the moment the twilight faded, predicting with no surprise the promise of a sleepless night, a latent feeling. Drunk on this complicit twilight, I allowed myself to be carried away by the fragrance of memories, the whispers of hours past, like a distant echo. Each star, gleaming like a forgotten jewel, stood watch—its light cutting through the darkness, safeguarding my restless thoughts.

The celestial vault, vast and impenetrable, confronted me with my reflections, inviting me to plunge into a bottomless introspection. The hours circled me, insidious and capricious, weaving a restless tapestry of anxiety and hope—as if the night itself conspired to deepen the silence of my thoughts. I knew then that sleep, that elusive companion, would not grace me with its soothing embrace this time.

An awakened world distinguished itself by its clarity, mingled with darkness. Each shade was a warning, each breath a persistent memory. Sometimes, the shadow of a fleeting dream would brush past me. The inaccessible then took form, only to disappear in the contact of reality. I remained with the bitter taste of the unfinished. I clung to this watchful lucidity, both salvational and torturous, prepared to welcome the day that, inevitably, would chase away my nocturnal contemplations.

Each exhalation held my own breath captive, caught in the uneasy wait for the next inhale. This fragile rhythm, punctuated by the feverish beating of my heart, gave the night a disjointed tempo—

stretching endlessly into the dark. Every second clung to the one before it as if time itself hesitated, floating in a thick ether, where reality became soft and malleable, bending to my anxieties.

In this interval between two breaths, I was both vulnerable and awake, aware of the depth of existence unfolding beneath my closed eyelids. The air, laden with the scents of the night, seemed to seep into me to nourish my reflections, feeding a fire of burning thoughts that longed to come to life. Twilight stood as a silent witness to my inner turmoil, etching into its depths the contrast between the suffocating weight of uncertainty and the aching desire to rise above it.

It was a ballet of anxiety and hope, where each breath imposed a question without an answer: what does this darkness conceal? What promises might emerge, shining brightly, when the light decides to pierce through the shadows? The tension, thick and undeniable, seeped into every fiber of my being—a stark reminder that in this fleeting world, breath and soul were inseparable, drawing me toward the unknown, the inexplicable.

Her exhalations threatened her departure, like the hesitant waves of a capricious ocean, while her inhalations gave me a fleeting sensation of promise, a spark of life clinging to hope. This illusion, sweet yet cruel, contrasted with the reality of her state—dark and unyielding. The despair of her passing had now been scheduled, measured in hours by the rigid gears of a medical machine, orchestrating a dark symphony through the chemical combination of a powerful anxiolytic. The cartridges, delivering their precise and unrelenting flow, dictated a six-hour wait between each injection—measuring the time left with mechanical certainty, an unyielding countdown.

Raphaël L. Marly

The small doses of morphine she received after each spasm provided relief mixed with unbearable pain. It was like a tragic alchemy, where the body, expressing its suffering, revealed deep truths that lay beneath a surface of apparent calm. Every movement, every spasm, was a betrayal of the anxiety that consumed her, a ballet in which she was forced to participate, with no say in the music. Though distant from me, her struggle was both tangible and elusive— a silent drama of unbearable intensity. Only fleeting moments of lucidity could glimpse it, revealing the quiet echo of her resistance against the inevitable.

Room 17

In this tension filled with emotions, I was confronted with the absurdity of life, with the fragility of existence—a taut thread wavering hesitantly between breath and "nothingness." Every minute became a thought, a muffled cry in the corners of my mind, obstructing the desire for clarity in the face of the inevitable darkness of her fate.

Sleep and I fought against each other in a confrontation where each beat of my heart rose like a lament of revolt against the desire to surrender to the arms of Morpheus. Like a sudden surge of hoped-for life, adrenaline—wild and untamed—climbed through me like a relentless vine, forcing me into a state of electrified wakefulness. It pulsed within me, defying sleep, giving me the illusion of vitality that only the circumstances allowed, while each minute slid slowly, forcing me to remain present, to fight against oblivion.

However, in this fierce struggle, I realized that my vigilance was not so much a conquest as the accompaniment of a final sigh. Watching over her, I stood guard through the night—witnessing the restless stirrings of her sleep, her fragility laid bare in the quiet anguish of her fading presence. Every movement of her body, every breath taken in the vacuity of time, was a tribute to the tenacity of life itself, even when everything seemed to fade away.

Her heartbeat, detached from any notion of what was unfolding, followed a rhythm that mixed despair with hope, drawing my thoughts into turbulent meanders. Adrenaline offered me a false sense of control, while in reality, I became the helpless witness to a battle with certain contours. The light of reason flickered, dimming beneath the weight of worry, as darkness slowly claimed the space we inhabited.

Raphaël L. Marly

I persisted in this vigilant watch, on the edge of wakefulness and dreams, aware that even if sleep eluded me, it offered, in turn, the possibility of discovering another form of intimacy, a communion between two souls looking into the infinity of the moment.

The seconds, the minutes, and the hours spent with her carried an unprecedented value, each one standing as a rare treasure within the insatiable river of time. It was as if each moment could latch onto the stage of eternity, taking on a particular dimension in the surrounding melancholy. I perceived every breath, every delicate movement, as a sacred gesture that piously honored our shared reality.

In this place that had become a sanctuary of tender moments, where the ordinary, the monotony of daily life disappeared, I measured the weight of these moments as one would assess precious stones, revealing facets that sparkled under the gaze of trembling love.

The present flowed like an impermanent fragrance, impregnating the room with a mysterious presence, both sweet and bitter, where the urgency of the moment confirmed the vulnerability of existence. Memories intertwined, creating a tapestry of tender and poignant images, a narrative with many voices where the past mingled with the imminent departure.

Thus, these moments, precious and dense, took the form of treasures buried in the corners of my memory, witnesses to a love that, though threatened, continued to shine in the growing darkness. I cherished the irreplaceable bond we shared, learning to recognize the quiet light that could still emerge, even from the depths of the night.

Like a capucinade, this awaited trial, initiated by the whisper of destiny, elevates our relationship with time and the people we cherish to another level. In this brutal clarity, the trivial transforms into the insignificant, while the essential, like a phoenix, illuminates itself in the lived experience alongside them. The others, those whose presence embellishes our existence, reveal themselves as bright stars in a moonless night, standing out with striking clarity in the shadow that surrounds us.

Chapter 10

The Promise of the Stars

"Life is both a dream and a reality, and
death is the end of the dream."

— Virginia Woolf

This communion in the depth of
the moment pushes us to reconsider how
we value our exchanges: shared laughter,
knowing silences—all of these take on a
new form, a resonance that dismantles the
illusion of eternity. Every glance became
a silent vow, every gesture a testament of
love, rooting our memories deep within
the fertile soil of our hearts.

Room 17

As time flows by, I realize that the essence of love is not reduced to the sum of encounters but is expressed in the richness of emotions experienced and the union of souls. Promises, often repeated in vain, lose their weight before the reality of shared moments, transforming routine into wonder. In the brilliance of the ephemeral, we learn to value each sigh, understanding that even fragility can harbor unexpected strength.

Thus, as life unfolds, we build bridges to those we cherish, transcending the trivialities of the everyday. This renewed perception of time, illuminated by love, turns each interaction into a gesture of authenticity—redefining priorities, sweeping away the insignificant, and revealing the quiet, undeniable beauty of what truly matters.

My mother's earthly love was transforming, manifesting itself in new forms, as if her soul needed to reinvent itself. My sensitivity mirrored the delicacy of a butterfly's wings, ready to be carried away by the gentlest breeze. Each second spent together was imbued with a particular intensity.

My mother's life expectancy had now morphed into a "lepidopteran" reality, evoking the fleeting beauty of butterflies admired in a fleeting instant before they take flight. This term, laden with meaning and emotion, reminded me that each day carried a unique significance that I must savor rather than take for granted. In this turmoil, life gained tangible meaning, each moment becoming a showcase of our unbreakable bond.

This transformation of our intimacy was an invitation to appreciate tenderness in vulnerability, to dive into the depth of every gesture, every word. The present enclosed the past, a witness to our laughter and shared confusion. Suddenly, everything took on a profound and powerful meaning. Time bent around us, teaching me to see love through a new lens—to embrace its fleeting nature and to treasure every moment of its presence.

Thus, I strove to capture these pearls of life—the essence of a love that, despite upheavals, continued to grow and evolve, wrapping me in infinite warmth and depth. In this space, I was learning not only to love but to appreciate every breath, every spark of life illuminating the end of our path.

The space between life and death became as perceptible as the Drake Passage or the Northwest Passage— where the Pacific and Atlantic Oceans seem not to mix on the surface yet merge in their unfathomable depths, uniting their waters in an invisible bond. A deep undercurrent, a silent tide flowing from one ocean to another—just as my mother, in her little sky-blue room, was gently drifting from the realm of the tangible into the embrace of the unseen. Each heartbeat, each breath, was one more step toward this imminent, almost imperceptible, yet inevitable transition.

Shortly before 6 a.m., the night began to yield to dawn. I rose before the day broke, folding up the cot that had been kindly set up for me the night before. Sleep had barely touched me, and the quick shower I took felt more like a ritual of awakening than a genuine necessity. The cold water ran over my skin as if to remind me of reality while my thoughts remained stubbornly fixed on the bed where she lay—the promise of a new day nothing more than a faint whisper.

During my brief time in the bathroom, I had to momentarily part with the rounded olive-wood cross I always kept clutched in the palm of my hand. Unsure of where to place it, I spoke to my mother in a soft murmur, gently explaining my intentions—as if seeking her silent guidance.

Room 17

"Mom, I'm going to leave the cross right next to you on your pillow."

I pictured it watching over her sleeping face, like a protective relic, as I imagined the Archangel Raphael leaning over her, saving her from her suffering and granting her respite, an extension of life. But he did not come, though he was so longed for.

"Mom, I'm leaving the cross by your side, on your pillow, while I shower. You'll stay with me, won't you?"

Yes, I spoke to her during that bleak, harsh night as if my words could weave a bond between us—a barely silent prayer to heaven to keep her with me a little longer. Every word felt like a thread connecting the present to eternity, hope to resignation, a fragile yet essential dialogue to endure the night.

Every second, every fleeting minute, seemed to take on monumental significance. Time had shrunk, fracturing into precious fragments. Each moment became a wellspring of anguish, and each wave of anguish solidified into inevitability. Part of me surrendered to this inescapable truth, while the other clung desperately to the fragile belief that where there is hope, life still lingers. This heart-wrenching duality accompanied me in every breath, every thought, every glance at her.

"Little Mom, I'm going to fold the blanket and the sheets now."

These simple, everyday words carried a strange solemnity in the silence of the room. Every action, every word, became an offering—a prayer to keep her tethered to this world for just a little longer.

I did not expect to have to turn as swiftly as the wind, interrupting the act of folding the navy blue blanket. Her breathing seemed to have paused once more—a breath held like a taut string, followed by an exhale that was not gasping but deep, almost endless, as if in farewell. She released her final breath, forgoing any future inhale. It was a moment of staggering intensity, a point where time seemed to freeze in an abyss of sorrow.

The experience consumed my entire being, overwhelming me with grief as I confronted the full weight of the phrase "To give up the ghost." Words I had often heard without truly feeling their depth now carried an unbearably stark reality. With cruel simplicity, they carried the weight of truth—the undeniable reality of this passage, the irreplaceable loss of a cherished presence.

Room 17

It was as if my mother's soul, having fulfilled its earthly journey, had freed itself to join an invisible realm, leaving behind an immense and immeasurable void.

Raphaël L. Marly

About The Author

Since the dawn of my seventeenth year, the desire to write has always been present, like a vital breath. As Raphaël L. Marly, I feel deep within me an irresistible urge to tell stories, reignited by the departure of my mother. Her absence opened a breach in my soul, pushing me to transcribe emotions and memories, to give voice to what remained unexplored. In this quest for writing, I have found refuge, a way to honor her memory and explore the twists and turns of my own being.